JC & Ros

Jane Harriett

2006

A Door to Christmas

A Door to Christmas

Robert M. Turner

VANTAGE PRESS
New York

Illustrated by Tanya Stewart

FIRST EDITION

Copyright © 1999, 2005 by Robert M. Turner

Published by Vantage Press, Inc.
419 Park Ave. South, New York, NY 10016

Manufactured in the United States of America
ISBN: 0-533-15214-3

Library of Congress Catalog Card No.: 2005903113

0 9 8 7 6 5 4 3 2 1

For Nancy . . .
Who makes it Christmas all year long

Contents

Gifts: Wanted or Needed

$\mathcal{A}$dele triumphantly affixed the tape on the sixth package that she had wrapped for mailing. She was on her way to get the labels when the phone rang. The conversation lasted longer than usual, but she indulged herself because she deserved it. Christmas gifts were always such a hassle for Adele, even though there were not that many names on her list. Since she had never been married, she felt so uneducated about what was pleasing to either men or children. She found women to be so picky that it made her nervous to shop for them.

However, she had absolutely outdone herself this year. She was confident that her six recipients would abound with joy. Each gift was just perfect, and she could imagine the countenance of her nineteen-year-old niece, a college student, when she opened her package.

Now, the niece thought that the whole world was a party and that such was the purpose for existence, so Adele gave her all the paraphernalia for a New Year's Eve party. What a giggly good time Adele had had in the party store, selecting hats, peanuts, napkins, invitations, mints, and confetti. Everything for

a fun evening was there. Adele did so not want to be thought of as "the old maid auntie." With pleased pride did she write the note to be enclosed:

Darling . . . Love life and share it with your friends on New Year's Eve.

Now Adele's own old maid aunt was quite another matter. She was the frail and delicate sort to whom one gave lilac sachet and lace handkerchiefs. Adele fingered the cameo broach one last time and held it to her cheek before she wrapped it. The broach had been an engagement gift from Adele's father to her mother. She had seen her mother wear the pin always, but somehow Adele was never quite comfortable wearing it. She knew her mother's sister would cherish the opportunity, so lovingly she wrote a little note to her aunt:

I received this from the greatest lady I have ever known and pass it on to the next great lady of our family.

Adele liked her pastor. For a long time, she had wanted to express her appreciation and affirm him in some way. When she saw the little volume entitled *Jesus and Alcohol,* she knew that would be a right gift because seldom did he preach a sermon without making reference to the subject. Total abstinence was one of his strongest tenets. The little inscription had a certain dignity about it. She wrote:

Your words and actions influence so many lives. Thank you for all the good you do and are.

Her boss was quite another matter. She had secretly been in love with him for three years, but he had not so much as called her by her first name. She wanted a gift that would say, "Hey, I'm interested," but one that would not indicate that she was being too friendly. A thirty-five-dollar gift certificate from a local department store seemed just the right messenger. Carefully she wrote on his card an innocuous: "Merry Christmas."

Adele's brother drank too much, especially since he had married that woman with all those children. He had commented that his home life was hell. She knew her pastor certainly would not have approved of the gift that she was sending to her brother; nevertheless, she had purchased a bottle of the most expensive bourbon. If it would bring her brother a few evenings peace and relaxation, it would be a good investment. Almost apologetically she wrote:

Hope this provides a little sanctuary all your own. Try it. You'll like it.

Finally she had wrapped the little teddy bear for her five-year-old nephew and wrote some sort of endearment that she felt would be comprehensible to someone of his age level. Yes, all in all, she was quite pleased with herself and her gifts for the year.

Adele finished her telephone conversation. She affixed the labels on the packages to be mailed. She sat back, put her feet up, and began to enjoy Christmas. It was a good feeling.

Three days later, at three o'clock in the afternoon to be exact, her world began to unravel. Her first hint of trouble was that Aunt Hattie was calling in the middle of the day instead of at night when the rates were cheaper. That could only mean that there was a death in the family or a real emergency. The old woman was so excited that her voice was shaky. "Adele, I've never done anything like that in my whole life, but if you think I should, I'll try. You must come and help. Can you get some more of those invitations?"

As the excitement rose in the spinster's voice, Adele slowly began to grasp that somehow the labels had gotten switched on the Christmas packages and that her aunt had received the party package and was going full speed ahead with plans for a New Year's Eve party. Adele could hardly keep back the tears and laughter, as she listened to her aunt planning her first party. She realized that there was a warm human being underneath the lilac and lace. Adele assured her aunt that she would be there to help.

She wondered who had received the broach, but no matter. After Christmas she would get it all straightened out. However, if Adele could have seen her pastor fondling the bottle of bourbon, she would have known that things were never to be straightened out again. Once again the man irately read the smart-aleck note attached, and he almost shouted,

"Who does Adele think she is? 'Have a little sanctuary all your own. Try it. You'll like it.' I've never had
a drink in my life." It might be noted that he slept
more soundly that night (far into the next morning,
in fact) than he had in many years.

Many people commented on how unusual it was
to send a five-year-old a thirty-five-dollar gift certificate. His mother said it was the most maturing thing
that could have happened to Timmy. He misunder-
stood what a gift certificate was and thought it had to
be spent on gifts for others. He had invested the entire afternoon in the store, thinking about gifts for
other people. The child learned much from Adele's
mistake, and Adele received much credit for being so
perceptive about the ways of children.

Her brother wrote Adele the strangest note. He
had received the book about alcohol, and mentioned
to her that he had not realized his drinking had gotten so bad that it was obvious to the whole family. He
said he had read the book twice and was going to join
AA, and he thanked her for being such a special sister.

Perhaps the only one deeply hurt by the mixups
was Adele's niece. The girl stood crying in her college
dormitory room as she held the cameo broach against
the red satin party dress. There was such a small
amount of material in the dress that there was no
place to pin the broach even if she had wanted to. No
two things could have been further apart than that
dress and the cameo broach.

Once again she read the inscription ". . . to the

6

next great lady of our family . . ." *After I spend the holidays with Jack in Mexico, no one will ever call me a great lady,* she thought. She had lied to her mother about not being able to come home for Christmas. She alibied with her work and studies. She clutched the broach in one hand and picked up the phone in the other, as she inquired of a bewildered mother, "I've changed my mind. Can I still come home for Christmas?"

Adele was never to know about a conversation between that mother and daughter, a conversation that lasted well into the night. However, Adele was to one day see that broach pinned to a wedding dress as a beautiful young lady walked down the aisle.

As Adele sorted through all that had happened, she realized that her boss must have received the teddy bear. He simply was not the sort of man to whom one sent a teddy bear. She thought of possible explanations and even went over in her mind what she might say to him. In fact, she decided that he might smile just a little bit about the matter . . . by Easter.

All day she tried to remember just exactly what she had written on the little card intended for her nephew. When the inscription did surface from the caverns of her mind, the color drained from her face and she took two of her strongest headache capsules. Well, she would simply have her resignation on his desk when he arrived Monday morning. There was no other way because she certainly could never look him in the eye again. Her note had read:

My dearest . . . I wish I could hug you as tightly as I know you will squeeze this bear. Come to see me and we will have a Christmas you will never forget.

Perhaps an act of God will disintegrate the stupid little card that was with that bear, Adele thought. *Or maybe the mail will lose the package.* However, there was no act of God. The mail did not lose the package. The telephone did ring.

"Adele?" greeted her boss. "What time did you want me to come over on Christmas?" Well, now there is the beginning of a beautiful friendship.

It was some Christmas, never to be forgotten. Nobody got what Adele had intended for them to have, but everyone had gotten just exactly what they needed. The love of God does work in mysterious ways, its wonders to perform.

The Ungiven Gift

*F*or seventy-eight years, Mollye had loved Christmas. She loved the smell of fir trees and the messiness of making fruitcakes. She loved the mysteries of locked closets and the notes on cards. She loved the sounds of song and the hugs of friends. She loved everything about Christmas, and it was Christmas that she missed most of all at the Happy Year's Nursing Home. She tried not to dwell on the inaccuracy of the name; instead, her thoughts had focused all fall on Christmas.

With determined movements her arthritic hands had painfully and painstakingly made the afghan. It was truly one of her best and the design was her own. Every time Miss Graham complimented her work, Mollye smiled because the afghan was to be a gift for the social worker who gave so much of herself to dispel the dismalness of the nursing home. No one ever gave to Miss Graham in return, and this gift was to say "Thank You" for three years of shopping for just the right threads and yarns that Mollye had required. It was the pleasure of anticipation that kept her fingers moving.

Her pastor had moved into a new home and

Mollye had beautifully pieced hot pads from shades of red and blue scraps gathered from anywhere she could find them for him. She had saved enough to have her dresser set with its Art Nouveau figures re-silvered to give to her daughter. For her grand-daughter, Mollye had carefully written out her favorite recipes and made it a little book of Christmas with cutouts from old cards. She included in it little bits of memories from Christmases past.

Reflecting upon her efforts, she was really proud of her accomplishments. All had been planned except for her son's, but something would emerge. Mollye's plans were matriculating methodically and she was loving all of it.

Now as social workers go, Miss Graham was tops, but perhaps too young to grasp the needs of a mature mind. Why could she not have accepted the afghan graciously? It would have pleased Mollye much to perceive of her young friend covered with her afghan on a cold winter afternoon reading a book. Nevertheless, the young woman insisted that she could not accept such a gift, and Miss Graham had placed Mollye's afghan with the others that were to go for sale at the Senior Citizen's Fair.

Maybe, if it does not sell, thought Mollye, *Miss Graham will take it then.* It sold. Mollye tried to act nice when the young woman brought her the seventy-five dollars, but it is difficult to hold back disappointment when a Christmas surprise had been rejected.

Well, at least, she would no longer have a problem about a gift for her son. He loved sports shirts by a certain designer. The shirts were about the same amount that Mollye had received for the afghan. It was a ridiculous price to pay, but Mollye would relish providing such an extravagance for her boy. She had fun finding a picture of such a shirt in a magazine, gluing it to an envelope, and placing the money inside. She was almost glad by the time his weekly visit rolled around on Sunday afternoon that the afghan had sold. He could get the shirt in time to wear it for Christmas, a red one. She would insist.

Her gift stunned the forty-five-year-old man. His mother had not had so much cash in years. Of course, he would not dream of accepting such a sacrifice from her and insisted that she use the money to get something for herself.

Her daughter had missed seeing the old dresser set on Mollye's chest and inquired about it. Mollye told a little Christmas lie and said that it had just disappeared, to which the daughter responded, "Oh, good. I've always hated those things."

The granddaughter never even came to get her gift because of the rush of Christmas on a college campus, but she promised to come before the New Year. Mollye simply never mentioned the hot pads when she heard about the new parsonage being decorated in all gold and green.

Before she went to bed that night, she carefully placed those ungiven gifts in the bottom drawer of her chest with the names still attached. It was her last touch of Christmas because that night Mollye slipped away to be with the one about whom Christmas evolves.

Mollye's daughter was bent with grief as she lifted the dresser set from its tissue. Ceremoniously she handed the homemade book to her own daughter who had finally come to the Happy Year's Nursing Home. The money and the hot pads still lay where Mollye's shaky hands had placed them.

Christmas Eve is a horrible time for a funeral. Not many came. The casket with its bright red bows and pine spray looked like a Christmas package unopened. Those closest to Mollye were all there, and they cried. How much better it would have been if instead of tears of grief they had been tears of joy for moments of happiness that Mollye had yearned to share.

The Holly Bush

$\mathcal{D}$ale stood at the door of his forty-year-old house and listened to the sad story of the Boy Scouts. It seems that they had sold more orders for bags of holly than they had produce to deliver. To make matters worse, they had already spent the money. Furthermore, it also seemed that Dale had the only holly bush in the neighborhood fully berried. They were desperate and Dale was not a Scrooge, but he simply could not allow them to cut his holly bush. The door closed on the negative negotiations and both parties felt badly.

Dale thought about the holly bush all day. It had been planted in anger fifteen years ago to keep a gate in the backyard from ever being opened again. They were all young then and their own children had been Boy Scouts. The two families were the closest of friends and the fence had been built with a connecting gate so that their backyards were as one and visiting was constant.

He couldn't even remember what the fight had been about. Perhaps several misunderstandings got blown out of proportion. What difference could it all make now anyway? The only thing he remembered

was seeing his friend put a lock on the gate. That very afternoon Dale had planted the holly bush, one with sharp edges that would hurt anyone who tried to get by it. As the bush had grown, so had the separation between the families. Occasionally over fifteen years, some overture of reconciliation had been made by one party or the other, but the hurt had never healed. Dale suspected most of it was his recalcitrance.

He didn't sleep very well that night and deep down in his heart he knew why. His breakfast was quietly shared with his wife. She seemed to sense that it was an important day. He simply asked her without explanation, "Do you know where my gloves are? This has gone on long enough." He made one brief phone call to a child and asked the Boy Scouts to be there in an hour.

His heart was pounding as he began to cut. Had the neighbors also planted hedges on their side? Was their tool shed still in front of the gate? How would he ever get his beautifully manicured backyard to look the same? He knew not the answers to these questions. He only knew that a bush of hatred had grown as long as it was ever going to grow in his backyard. It was time for something bad to be transformed into something good.

As the giant bush began to thin, Dale scarcely had the nerve to glance toward the neighbor's house. When he did, he could not believe what he saw. A long time ago someone had not only removed the lock, but the gate was also gone. A carefully mani-

16

cured path led to the neighbor's back door and a mat which said WELCOME on the other side of the fence led to a life of newness and love.

Baptized by Christmas

$\mathscr{T}$ed stared out the window of his elaborate office at the cold winter day. He wished that he had left earlier because then the telephone call and the invitation to share a ride to the event could have been avoided, but it was too late now and the arrangements had been made. Jack's invitation was not an indication that Ted's companionship was wanted. What Jack really wanted was to show off his new Mercedes. Even though they had shared vice president's positions in the same corporation for many years, there had never been any love lost between them. In fact, they probably would have killed each other long ago had it not been for their third counterpart, Gilbert, who had a neutralizing personality and the trio had productively kept the corporation profitable for two decades.

There had even been friction and competition among them about the gifts they would take to the baptism. It was the boss's first grandchild. Careful selection was called for; besides, they had all watched the boss's daughter, Carol, grow up and they were all fond of her. Jack was giving a hundred shares of company stock. He had no family and could

afford to do that. His gifts were always flashy and showy. Everyone would know about the impressive gift because he would, no doubt, pass the certificate around the baptismal ceremony.

Gilbert had chosen a lifetime subscription to *National Geographic Magazine*. Ted's funds were more limited and he hoped his gift would not seem inappropriate. Much thought had gone into the selection of the twenty-five compact discs and the modest system on which they could be played. He tried to remember recordings that his own children had loved. At least he had a wrapped package to take, which was more than the others.

They would need to leave early because none of them had ever been to the country church before and the Christmas traffic might be heavy. Heretofore, all family ceremonies had been held at the cathedral. Carol's baptism had been at that cathedral on Christmas Eve twenty years ago. Ted smiled as he remembered the modest gifts that the three of them had proffered at that gathering. Here they were on Christmas Eve twenty years later, gathering for the same purpose. The governor's daughter had scheduled the cathedral for her wedding that afternoon. Thus it had been decided that the current baptism would be at the baby's father's home church in a neighboring farm community.

The drive was frosty in more ways than one. Jack was enthralled with his new car. Gilbert was miffed that his entire family had not been invited. Ted sat in the back seat, thinking how much he disliked both of them. He hoped that they would not ask what was in his enormous package.

Ted need not have worried about the size of his gift because it took second place to the Shetland pony, which the workers' union had in a trailer outside the little country church. The poor taste of the working class, as usual, offended Ted. How could they? At least the shipping department had sent a puppy. All in all, it was some array. Management and labor trudging into the church together was almost funny to Ted since the strike was rumored to be next week and swearing had been their only tool of communication lately.

Well, there they were, an odd assortment of people and gifts, if one ever existed. The young pastor, unnerved by all the prominence and strangeness, kept apologizing for his overcrowded little church and its lack of heat. When he asked them to join in the singing of "Silent Night" a capella, there was almost a negative reaction, but they did. Those gruff, angry voices, those voices of parental love, and those knowing, aged voices of grandparental perspective all blended into goodness.

As the pastor took the baby, a ray of light from a stained-glass window was cast on them both. It was more than beautiful: it was hopeful: it was fresh loveliness. Ted remembered the baptism of his own children, as he secretly brushed a tear from his cheek. He felt his soul swelling inside of him. Why did people have to hate and put each other down and have so much greed? Why could life not be refreshing and clean, just as it was at that moment?

The caterers had evidently gotten lost because they never showed with the buffet that had been ordered. A Girl Scout group, having their little party in a Sunday school room, offered to share their refreshments. Jack had never tasted Kool-Aid and asked if it were some sort of country drink. Miraculously, they seemed to have enough.

The baby was passed from arm to arm and loved and admired. Labor and management even laughed and visited as they passed the cookies and stirred up more Kool-Aid. Ted even enjoyed riding home in Jack's new Mercedes.

As he got out of the car, impulsively he asked, "By the way, Jack, if you have no plans for Christmas dinner, would you like to share with us?" Jack simply turned his face away from Ted, but he nodded acceptance.

As he walked away, Ted wondered what in the world would be the future of a baby who had such a strange beginning.

The Advent Investment

The door slammed hard as Carol left the psychologist's office, but she could have cared less. In her own mind, she had been pondering the validity of the expensive sessions, and today had finalized her decision. No longer would she pay twenty-five dollars a session just to be insulted. She did not need to pay someone to tell her that she needed to get involved with people. She knew that. The problem was how to get involved.

It was a sign in a store window that had first seeded the venture in Carol's imagination. It probed: "Are you willing to spend a dollar a day to save a life?"

Well, why not? she thought. Already she had set aside twenty-five dollars for her next session. She just might give the money to the advertised charity. However, she decided to invest a dollar a day in her own life. There were about twenty-five days left until Christmas. She already had that many dollars tucked aside. Under those circumstances, the plan was conceived.

Already she was three days behind schedule since it was December 3, but no matter! By the time

she got back to her office, the first installment of her investment was planned. The dowdy divorcée who worked at the desk next to Carol's was always trying to sell something for one of the organizations in which her children participated. This morning the product had been candy bars for the junior high band. Carol had never been fond of the co-worker, and the selling had always irritated her. In fact, that very morning Carol not only had refused to buy the candy, but had curtly reminded her co-worker, "This is a business office and not a confectioner's stand."

It did Carol good to apologize for her earlier rudeness. She even bought three of the candy bars with the first three dollars of her investment. The seller, anxious to smooth things over, offered an explanation. "I feel so guilty about not being more involved with my children. Maybe they will know that I am supporting them if I can help in this way. Thank you for understanding, Carol."

So, investing dollars 1, 2, and 3 in candy bars, Carol wrote three little notes, which read: "Merry Christmas from a Friend," and she placed them in the mailboxes of the three bachelors who worked in the office. She was confident that her investment would produce three big smiles and looks of endearment, which they did, but not to Carol. The three receiving bachelors all thought the coworker had given the candy to them, so they smiled at her. The co-worker had a lovely, friendly afternoon without ever knowing the motivating impetus of her newly found popularity.

Carol was a bit miffed about her first investment, to say the least. Her bad mood caused her to invest dollar 4 in a can of dog food. For weeks a neighbor's dog had howled nocturnally. Her tacky note on the dog food read: "Merry Christmas to your dog, who must be very hungry, else he would not keep the entire building awake all night." That on the threshold did the trick and a special gift of sleep was thereby given to an entire building.

Dollars 5 and 6 sponsored two beautiful Christmas cards. One was sent to a high school civics teacher who had taught Carol how to read the newspaper. The other went to a local TV news broadcaster whose candor and accuracy Carol had always found helpful. Carol was amazed to realize how many people had contributed to her enjoyment of life. Just to be on the safe side, she made a list of other people to whom she could send cards just in case her dollar investment ideas ran slow.

Appropriately enough, dollar 7 came up on a Sunday. Carol dreaded being exposed to another dull, boring sermon. The pastor was capable of brilliance and occasionally let it sparkle, but usually his homilies were more akin to an endurance contest. Great preaching for the rest of the month would certainly be worth a dollar. Carefully did she work the anonymous telegram he was to receive.

Thought it unfair for you not to know that the pulpit committee from a large church will be in your services for the next three Sundays.

For her second week of investments, Carol dedicated herself to a united project, each day's dollar being a part of the whole. The apartment house in which she lived was poorly kept and unfriendly, typical of non-resident management. No one ever spoke. Vulgar graffiti would stay on the wall around the mailboxes for months. Carol had never even seen several of the twenty residents in the building, but she was planning to know all of them by Saturday night.

Dollar 8 was spent on a poster proclaiming the holiday party for all building residents, Saturday night at 7:00 P.M. in the lobby. She taped the poster to the front door. Dollar 9 was spent on little notes dropped into each mail box, telling the invited what they were to bring to the party. She double-assigned all foodstuffs just in case some did not show. The notes were signed, "Your Party Committee." Dollar 10 brought a red ribbon for the wreath that she had made from free tree trimmings. Hanging above the mail boxes, it served as a daily reminder, especially since the attached greeting read, "Merry Christmas from Your Party Committee."

Dollar 11 saw two fresh candles go into the holders glued to the entrance hall table. As far as anyone knew, it was the first time they had ever been filled. She would light them on Saturday night. Dollar 12 purchased a box of mints to place between the candles. It was the first complimentary things some of the city dwellers had been offered in years. Carol smiled to see three of the doorways of the drab building boasting some sort of decoration for the first time ever.

Dollar 13 was really her brainstorm. She cleared the bulletin board and posted a stick-on name tag with the name of each resident. Acquiring the names had been no small task. She felt the name tags for the party would really commit them to appear, especially being posted a day in advance.

Dollar 14 underwrote a spray can of detergent. Carol situated herself in the lobby, scrubbing away the vulgarities and washing the windows. To all who came or went, she greeted, "See you at the party tonight."

Saturday night finally came and so did the residents. To say that it was the social event of the season would be an overstatement. Nevertheless, people met and talked and had a good time. One elderly man said that he had not been invited to a party in years, and another retired resident had obviously been working on her looks all week. People were no longer strangers, but individuals with names. Who would have believed it? Right there in her own building? She was exhausted!

Carol certainly had no intention of week three being another major undertaking, but it was certainly turning out that way. It had all begun at church that morning when the pastor, who incidentally preached the most fantastic sermon you ever heard, asked members of the congregation to visit the shut-in members. There was one name not far from where Carol lived, so she took it and even invested Dollar 15 in a small ivy plant to begift her fellow church member.

The address proved to be a third-rate nursing home that smelled when you walked in the front foyer. The old woman whom she had gone to see took one look at the ivy plant and snorted, "Why did you bring me that when what I really wanted was a goldfish?" The bluntness of senility was something to which Carol was not usually exposed, but as she eyed the empty fish bowl and a half-used box of fish food, Carol realized the old woman was in dead earnest. Dollar 16 brought a squiggling new resident to the cherished fish bowl, and a tired old resident was thrilled to experience the pride and authority of ownership once again.

Nevertheless, the church member's roommate was not quite so thrilled at the attention her partner was receiving. No one had brought her any gifts from her church. In not too subtle ways, she let it be known that what she would like to have for Christmas was a manicure. One quick glance told Carol that the woman really needed one.

"Don't you have any relatives or friends who visit and do that sort of thing for you?" Carol inquired. It was difficult for Carol to believe that neither of the women had received a card or visit from anyone in months, even though the roommate had two nephews and the other had a sister and two grandchildren.

Dollar 17 was spent on fingernail polish "HOT PINK" and an emery board. Dollars 18, 19, and 20 were spent on five get-well cards. The cards were not for the old ladies, but for their five errant relatives. The message on each read:

> Your relative here has asked me to send you a get-well card. She is convinced you are ill since it has been so long since she had heard from you. She is fine and spends most of her time with her lawyers writing her will. The large inheritance she recently received is proving to be a large responsibility.
>
> She sends her love and best wishes for a Merry Christmas.
>
> Her friend,
Carol

She then marked out "Her friend" and substituted, "Her dearest friend." Carol smiled, satisfied that the matter of loneliness for two old ladies had now been handled adequately.

Dollar 21 was invested quite by accident, as Carol stood waiting for a bus. She noticed a child fumbling for a quarter for a gumball machine. Parents are willing to part with pennies for such a cause, but a quarter brings a negative response. As she gave the little boy a quarter, two little girls grew closer. Finally she had spent all her change on any child who wanted it. Where else could you find so much happiness for a dollar? "Those children will smile every time they pass a gumball machine for the rest of their lives," Carol decided happily.

Dollar 22 proved not to be such a good idea. She had purchased a little booklet on good telephone manners and left it on her boss's desk. Often he was quite rude to Carol on the phone, but he had never offended her quite as much as when she found the booklet on her desk the next morning with the comment, "Thought you could use this."

Dollar 23 was invested in a long-distance call to an old neighbor. Carol had difficulty in controlling her emotions when the friend from another era of her life commented, "Oh, Carol, I was just sitting here feeling sorry for myself and thinking that no one in the whole world cared if I lived or died." Carol decided that might have been her best investment.

Dollar 24 would run a close race for producing happiness and alleviating loneliness. Carol baked two loaves of fresh bread and took them to the two older residents whom she had met at the apartment party. Never was any gift-bearing guest more welcome. It was good to be warmly, joyously, welcomed anywhere.

Dollar 25 and Christmas Eve finally surfaced. She wanted her last investment to be special and therefore had given a great deal of thought to the matter. The selection was carefully made and adorned with a festive red ribbon. The best one could do was to make the investment and hope the dividend would be forthcoming. All morning the other girls in the office had glared jealously at the dollar's worth of mistletoe that was hanging over Carol's desk. Dollar 25 provided a day of improving office relationships for Carol.

All in all it had been quite an advent for Carol.

Had twenty-five dollars ever produced so much? People in her building were speaking to each other. The congregation was being uplifted by the most glorious sermons they had ever heard. Two old ladies in a nursing home were being showered with attention from enthusiastic relatives. Children had smiled and friendships had been formed. On Christmas Eve, Carol had been hugged five times, kissed twice, and pinched once. All that for just twenty-five dollars.

She wondered if next year she started a little earlier and saved $100 . . .

Chad, Who Couldn't Understand

*C*had really wasn't a bad boy. It was just that he was nine years old and awkward. He never could quite really understand where adults were coming from, especially his parents. He had a big heart; in fact, it was the bigness of his heart that precipitated all the controversy over the smoked turkey that Aunt Mabel had sent them for Christmas. Chad had given it away. Without discussing the matter with any living human being, he had simply taken the smoked turkey to the church and placed it in the food barrel for needy families.

Chad believed that was a good thing to do since they already had two Christmas turkeys. His mother had bought one and his father's office had given them another. How could three people eat three turkeys? His dad claimed he hated smoked turkey. His mother moaned that there was no more room in the freezer. Chad's understanding was that he was solving three problems at once, counting the one about the hungry people, with his action of the gift of the smoked turkey. But then, Chad seldom understood.

He might have gotten by with the whole caper if Aunt Mabel had not written that she was coming for

Christmas dinner. Since she was very sensitive about the gifts she gave, Chad's mother had gone to the church to retrieve the much given turkey. She slipped in the side door, thinking no one would see her in that forlorn part of the building on a Thursday afternoon, but with the turkey in hand, she bumped into the preacher. How does a prominent woman in the community explain to the reverend why she is stealing a turkey from the poor barrel?

There may have been many things that Chad did not understand, but what he did understand was all the yelling and anger when his mother got home. He understood that he had done something terribly wrong, but he was not at all sure what it was, even though there seemed to be no doubts in his mother's mind about the matter.

Chad had something of the same confusion when his mother discovered that he had invited the Brown family for Christmas dinner. They had just moved into town and had a boy in Chad's room at school. When Chad learned that they were to spend Christmas in a motel room because their furniture had not yet arrived, he did what he thought was decent and invited them over.

Chad's mother's note to the Browns had been at best polite, as she explained that they had other plans for Christmas dinner, but they would look forward to getting together with them at some future date. Her note to Chad had a different tenor, which definitely was not harmonious. She made him stay in his room for a week after school with no TV. Chad could not understand what he had done that was so wrong.

Christmas Eve finally rolled around and things had calmed down somewhat. It was just about to be joyous until Chad's father stormed in the front door. It seems a representative from Boy's Ranch had visited him in the afternoon to collect the one hundred dollars that had been pledged for their Christmas party. Chad's father claimed he had made no such pledge and was somewhat chagrined when the solicitor produced a pledge card with the amount circled and properly initialed. To save further embarrassment, he had paid the pledge. Now he was demanding to know why Chad's mother had made such a commitment without consulting him. She had not. However, someone at that residence had initialed the computer card and returned it. Since Chad was the only other person living in that residence. . . .

Well, on Christmas Eve, Chad was spanked and sent to his room. "Deck the Halls" could be heard playing on the radio in the background.

The scenario in that home on Christmas Eve was less than Christmas card subject matter. Little happiness was to be found in the mess in the kitchen, as Chad's mother cleaned out the deep freeze in order to squeeze two more turkeys into its caverns. In fact, there was so much clutter in the kitchen that the family had to eat in the dining room. The five empty chairs at the table, which seated eight, gave the room an even gloomier mood. As was their custom, they bowed their heads for a brief prayer.

Chad's father was still so angry that he could not even close his eyes for the prayer. " . . . a hundred dollars to strangers," he mumbled. At least it would help at income-tax time. Anger, hostility, and frustration formed the trinity that hovered over the confused bowed heads. His father began the same old rote prayer he had prayed a thousand times without anyone ever paying attention to it. The rambling ritual went, "Thank you, Lord, for these gifts that we are about to receive. Bless the hungry, sick and needy . . . " but before he got to the "amen," his eyes fell on the kitchen table so covered with food from the deep freeze that much of it was having to be discarded. He looked at those five empty chairs around the dining table, and he thought of a family eating in the loneliness of a motel room. Most of all, he gazed at a nine-year-old boy with tear streaks still on his face, who had been yelled at, scolded, and spanked on Christmas Eve all for trying to live up to a prayer that he had heard his father pray a thousand times. Could this child who never understood anything have the only real understanding in the household?

The "amen" just simply would not come out of his father's lips. Perhaps it was the emotion of Christmas Eve, perhaps something else, but the father left the table abruptly and walked over to the Christmas tree with his back to the family. Chad did not understand.

"Is Dad crying because he knows God is not going to answer those prayers?" Chad asked his mother.

"No, Chad," his father proclaimed, as he picked up one of those frozen turkeys. "I'm crying because I know God is just about to answer them all. Get your coat on and let's go!" And at last, there was something that Chad understood.

Oscar

There was not much Christmas celebration anywhere in 1929, but the little church in Silverton, Texas, had donned its best party attire, even if it was homemade. There was a tall, gangly tree with a few candles and an abundance of paper chains. In the other corner was a punch bowl surrounded with a meager offering of cakes and cookies. Behind the piano was the biggie, because there were the treats that Santa Claus would give out at the appropriate moment. Each child under twelve would be gifted with a red net sack containing an apple and an orange, a few nuts and three peppermint canes. Many of the children only had fresh fruit at Christmas and the merchants had donated to the best of their ability. In the past there had been more, but this was the start of the Depression. Jake had built the fire in the old wood stove in the middle of the afternoon so that the drafty old building would be comfortable, and then he retired to try and make the ancient Santa Claus costume look presentable. They had done their best.

Everybody came. There was nothing else to do. They sang carols and had a good time and the antici-

pated moment finally arrived when the jingle of rein-
deer bells was heard and Jake in the midst of glory
appeared in the Santa Claus attire. No one laughed
out loud, but a few snickers were muffled around the
room. The sacks were distributed in a whirlpool of
confusion. After all the children had received their
treats, there were always a few gifts under the tree
for very special people. There was usually a gift for
the preacher and some homemade goodies for the
schoolteachers. The prettiest girls might receive a
couple of cards with a handkerchief or a bottle of
twenty-five-cent perfume. Nothing was ever very
spectacular, especially this year. However, there was
one rather impressively large gift left remaining
tucked far under the tree. A look of surprise was reflected even beneath Santa's beard when the name
on the package was discerned to be that of Oscar.

Oscar was mentally retarded. He was allowed to
attend school, but little more was ever expected of
him except to dust the erasers and empty the trash.
He also kept the woodbin filled if the teacher would
show him a little special attention. Needless to say,
much of the time he was the recipient of teasing and
sometimes even cruel actions. Never, however, had
Oscar experienced a moment as grand as when
Santa Claus handed him the fancy package. All eyes
in the room were watching. Who could have been so
thoughtful and generous? A more careful observer
might have spied three fifth-grade boys peering over
the back pew with their hands over their mouths, almost in uncontrollable laughter. It was a high mo-

ment in Oscar's history and people tended to share with him the anticipation as he awkwardly opened the gift. No one was more attentive to the opening of the package than Abe, Oran, and Bill.

When you have never received a special gift before, every nuance of the experience is to be filed away for future enjoyment. Slowly, Oscar opened the package and people leaned forward to catch a glimpse, but as they saw, repulsion spilled across their faces. In the package were three pig's feet. As the box was opened, the smell of rot was dominant where a few moments ago there had been the aroma of oranges and coffee. There is simply no way to describe the look on Oscar's face as he realized that he was simply the butt of one more prank. He never said a word. He gently placed the feet in the stove so that the smell would be killed and then slowly walked out the back door of the old church. He did not even stay for refreshments.

The party broke up soon after that. The festive mood was killed. What had happened was very much against the whole spirit of Christmas. What three cruel boys had thought would be funny was, in fact, blasphemy against the entire season and even the meaning of the church. The act had disgusted people. Everyone discussed who could have done that, but no one really wanted to know. It was a travesty against decency.

Three fifth-grade boys did not sleep very well that night. They really were not bad boys, just thoughtless. It was their intention for people to laugh, not get hurt; nevertheless, hurt had occurred. Early the next morning, Abe, who was really the leader of the three, slipped out of his house and rode his bicycle to the shabby house in which Oscar lived. Abe simply hung his sack of fruit and candy from Santa Claus on the doorknob and left. We do not know if Oscar found it or not. Neither do we know how he may have interpreted a second gift.

Oran denied vehemently to his mother that he was a part of the prank, but both knew the truth. That afternoon he bumped into Oscar downtown, and risking his reputation forever, he offered to pay Oscar's way into the movie. This meant that there would be no soda and popcorn for Oran, but somehow it made him feel better and Oscar seldom got to go to the picture show.

Bill was perhaps the most sensitive of the three. He simply could not shake the uneasy feeling. Every time the incident was referred to around the community, he felt a pang of regret. What had they been thinking about? They simply were not thinking at all. Bill had been coveting a wool jacket in the window of J.C. Penney's for some time. He knew that was to be his main present because the jacket had disappeared the same day that the gift wrapped with red and white striped paper with the black stagecoaches had appeared under their tree. He asked his mother if he could give the unwrapped gift to Oscar.

"Well, son, if that is what you really want to do, I guess it is all right, but let me discuss it with your father tonight," she responded. And that is what happened. Bill did not admit that he was making amends, but wise parents realized his need.

Maybe some good came out of the mistake after all. In any case, three boys made a special effort to see that Oscar's life was more pleasant. They certainly learned something about the spirit of Christmas and what makes people feel good and what hurts. Early in life they were learning that it is not a pleasurable thing to be on the side of hurt. All's well that ends well.

But Oscar never came to the Christmas party at the church again.

The Strong Box

$\mathcal{T}$he worn-out old house had a certain nostalgia about it. Bill could almost sense a warmth that was once there. He had lived there over a week now and was still in somewhat a state of surprise that he had taken every cent he had and purchased the modest old home lock, stock, and barrel. The previous owner had no heirs. Even her clothing and dishes and last year's canning were there. It was a strange collection of the possessions of a lifetime. He wondered how she would feel about his being there. He was almost hesitant to open drawers lest he invade her privacy. Nevertheless, it had to be done.

It was in the process of cleaning and moving and rearranging that he discovered the strong box mounted in the wall behind the china cabinet. His imagination absolutely ran wild about the probable contents. Jewels and debenture bonds and gold coins swirled in his dreams both waking and sleeping. Try as he might, he could not open the simple safe. He played with the combination almost every day. Finally in desperation, he engaged the services of a locksmith.

Inside the box were not the tangible assets about

which he had dreamed, but an odd assortment of trivia, which must have had meaning to the previous owner. There was an old magazine of a Christmas issue of *Better Homes and Gardens,* a letter with a twenty-five-year-old ticket stub from the Philadelphia Philharmonic, and an inexpensive little bracelet for a baby with the inscription of "Mary Jane" on it. Bill paid the locksmith and sat down with a cup of coffee to ponder his newly found cache. None of it made any sense. Why would anyone keep such trivia in a strong box? He started to throw it all away but instead took the yellowed letter from its envelope. The writing was the strong script of a young man. It read as follows:

Darling,

It is so wonderful to know that you are in the USA at last. My parents refuse to acknowledge our marriage, but they do adore Mary Jane. Their hatred of the Germans is deep. Please use the enclosed ticket to meet me at the Philharmonic Sunday afternoon and we will work out all the details of our new life together.

Love forever,

Bill reflected on the contents of the strong box for a while, even thumbing through the old magazine, and then carefully replaced them in the strong box and put the china cabinet back in place.

The cleaning and sorting procedures in Bill's new abode went slowly. It was difficult to sort through another person's possessions, even though they now belonged to you. There were many antiques and it was an old Dresden teapot that kept tugging at his mind. For some reason he felt an affinity with that piece of old china. He even dreamed about it one night. As he washed it and placed it back in the china cabinet, he thought that he remembered where he had seen it previously. Quickly he retrieved the old magazine from the strong box and there he found the picture of a woman holding the teapot over a festive holiday table. It was from an article entitled "A German Christmas Remembered." It was all about a German war bride and the few family pieces she had brought with her from Germany as well as recipes of the old country.

As he studied the laden table in the photograph, he realized that it was his table, and that most of the appointments on the table were things he had found in the house, even to the eyelet tablecloth. Now Bill knew why the old magazine had been kept. In fact, he felt it was a treasure of his house. He thought about trying to recreate the table with its sumptuous dishes, but he neither knew how to cook nor whom to invite to share such festivities with him.

As time went by, he reflected more and more on the other contents of the strong box. Were they too of equal significance? Was the woman to whom the letter was sent the one in the magazine? Why the ticket stub and the baby bracelet? Such ponderings caused him to do a very illogical thing. One afternoon he put the baby bracelet in a heavy envelope and addressed it to "Mary Jane" and sent it to the return address on the envelope of the old letter.

Five days later on a cold snowy afternoon, there was a knock on the door. Bill was startled because there had been no visitors in his new home. He was even more startled when he opened the door and found standing there a beautiful young woman who was a carbon copy of the woman in the magazine. She was holding the tiny bracelet in her hand and inquired blatantly, "Did you send this?"

Somewhat embarrassed now by his impromptu action, he invited her in and told in detail the drama of finding the strong box and how he had thought the little bracelet might be an important piece of nostalgia significant to someone at the address he had found. It was with a certain hesitancy in her voice that she asked if she might see the other contents of the box. Of course, he obliged.

She read the note and fingered the ticket stub carefully, but when he opened the magazine to the photograph, soft tears began to flow. She read the article and for a long time, there was only silence between them. Then with sacred deliberation, she whispered, "I think this was my mother and I have never seen a picture of her before."

Mary Jane told Bill that she had been reared by her grandparents. Her father had been killed in an automobile accident when she was only a baby. She knew that she had been brought from Germany right after World War II by her father, but she had been told that her mother wanted nothing to do with her and had simply given her to the father. She picked up the ticket stub and pointed to the date. "Bill, that was the date my father was killed. He was on his way to the Philharmonic when the accident occurred."

When the bracelet arrived addressed to her at the old family home, she had confronted her grandparents with questions, and they had finally admitted that they knew her mother had come to the USA. They had hired a lawyer to find the immigrant and inform her that both her husband and daughter had been killed in the accident and that there was no legal claim for her on the estate. Mary Jane said, "All my life I have been haunted by the fact that I thought my mother did not care about me. Now I know she was grieving for me. This little bracelet and what it symbolizes means everything in the world to me. I will never be the same." She gave Bill a little hug as she rose to leave.

Well, how did Bill respond? Did he give her the magazine? Did they have tea out of her mother's tea pot? Did she ever forgive her grandparents? Did she try to find some family in Germany? Did she blossom into a new person, knowing that her mother had cared? We do not know. That part of the story is missing. Your guess is as good as mine.

All we know for sure is that many years later when that strong box was opened again, those same articles were found in it. There was the baby bracelet showing some wear, the letter and the ticket stub greatly faded, and the old magazine almost in shreds from so much thumbing. However, there was one added article. It was an invitation to the wedding of someone named Bill and Mary Jane.

Why would anyone want to keep such old junk?

The Wrong Number

*G*eff stood stunned with the note from his grand-mother in his hands. Thirteen-year-old boys do not cry, but he brushed his eyes nevertheless. It was the first time that she had ever rebuked him. He reread her note again:

Dear Geff,

Your Christmas list has been received. I have seen catalogs with fewer items. I do not plan to give you a single one of those things. Instead, I want something from you. Please send me a list of what you plan to give to observe the birth of our Lord.

Love,
Grandmother

Geff, angry and embarrassed by her note, knew deep down in his heart that she was right. The matter was in his thinking for the rest of the day.

He thought of all sorts of typical things that a kid could do of a benevolent nature, but nothing really materialized. It all seemed rather trite actually.

The next day he decided to share the matter

with his girlfriend, but he was greeted on the other end of the phone by a strange older voice, "Miss Beasley here."

"Is this 927-5959?"

"No," came the older woman's voice, "This is 927-5958. I should have known it was a wrong number if my phone rang. No one ever wants to talk to me."

Geff apologized, but her comment lingered on in his thoughts, as well as did her voice. Finally, he remembered where he had heard the voice before. There was a certain familiar quality about it that nudged his memory. Finally, he remembered where he had heard the voice before, and he smiled as he dialed her number again.

"Miss Beasley here."

"Is this the Miss Beasley who used to read stories to children at the library on Saturday mornings?"

"Yes," she answered, "and to whom am I speaking?"

"This is Geff Stewart. You probably do not remember me, but I wanted to call and thank you for all those good times."

"Of course, I remember you, Geff, and would you believe that you are the first one to ever call and say thanks. It is so appreciated." They had a nice friendly sort of chat, which ended with an unexpected question.

"Geff, I have been in a wheelchair for about a year and can no longer leave my apartment. Would you like to earn some spending money by doing a few errands and chores for me?"

And so it began. After school two or three days a week, Geff did whatever Miss Beasley desired. He replaced bulbs, washed her front windows so that she could see the people in the street, rearranged her kitchen cabinets so that items often used could be reached from the wheelchair, and bought Christmas cards and stamps for her. It almost sounded as if she were thinking up chores for Geff as the two developed a rather unusual friendship.

When Geff arrived one afternoon, Miss Beasley commented, "I have been on the phone most of the day answering questions for people about children's books. It felt so good to be of use again."

"Good!" responded Geff, hoping that she would never know about the notice he had placed in the children's section of the local bookstore, which read:

FOR INFORMATION AND GIFT SUGGESTIONS
CALL MISS BEASLEY, CHILDREN'S LIBRARIAN
927-5958

One afternoon she told Geff that she had always loved the holiday *kolaches* from a certain pastry shop about two blocks away and would he mind running down there and purchasing some for her and her neighbor. Much to her surprise, he responded that he did mind and that she could get them for herself if she wanted them.

Astonished, she replied, "Why, Geff, I have not been out of this apartment for seven months."

To which he replied with a grin, "Can you get down those three front steps?"

"Well, I suppose I could," said Miss Beasley.

"Then, let's go get the *kolaches.*"

So an old woman in a moth-eaten fur coat in a wheelchair and a kid in tennis shoes made a funny sight on a glorious winter afternoon. It was the first of several excursions.

One afternoon, Geff wheeled her by the Kiwanis Christmas lot and began to roll her along the wide rows.

"What are we doing here?" she queried.

"Getting you a tree," the impudence of his youth responded.

"Now, Geff, I have not had a Christmas tree in fifteen years."

"Then," said Geff, "we had better select a big one to make up for lost time." People turned and laughed at the pilgrimage of the old woman with the red scarf holding the modest tree in her lap, being pushed by a youth whose demeanor reflected that of a statesman on a sacred mission.

What an afternoon that turned out to be! She told Geff where to find some antique decorations long since packed away and entertained him with tales of their origins and her former holidays.

Christmas Eve finally arrived and Geff and Miss Beasley exchanged gifts. He had bought her a new mystery that she had commented on in a store window and she had a special envelope for him with a generous cash gift. As he left, she thanked him for the nicest holiday season that she had experienced in many years.

As he left, himself happier than he had been in a long time, he neglected to lock the door of her apartment as he always did. The city took on the quiet of Christmas Eve and it was about midnight that an intruder quietly slipped open the door of Miss Beasley's apartment. He carried a pillow, a bag of kitty litter, and six cans of cat food, carefully arranging them around the tree. When it was to the intruder's satisfaction, he reached into his jacket and pulled out the ugliest kitten that God had ever allowed to be created. His ears were too big, his nose was too long, and his coat too mottled. In fact, his only redeeming feature was the bright red ribbon around his neck, one end of which was tied to the basket. The kitten assumed princely possession of the basket as the intruder slipped out the door. This time Geff locked it.

The next day at Christmas dinner his grandmother inquired of him, "Geff, I requested you to send me a certain list, but I never received it."

"Well, Grandmother, I was going to, but I dialed the wrong number," replied Geff with a tone indicating the end of the conversation.

"Really?" she replied. She thought to herself as she studied the twinkle in his eye, *He may have dialed the wrong number, but he found the right spirit.*

Ruby

$\mathcal{S}$et-up day is never easy at an antique show, and the old couple in Booth 307 had made it more difficult, even embarrassing, for their neighbors by personal and intimate arguments. Ruby and Larson were real authorities in the generation of conflict. The already too tight curls in her home perm seemed to become more inflexible as she accused him of dragging her away from home during the holiday season, and he cruelly responded by reminding her that it had been her decision not to have children so that they had neither reason to stay at home nor kin to prepare for anyway. His tall, gaunt figure with its deliberate and calculated movements reflected his recalcitrant spirit.

If she put an oyster plate on a top shelf, he immediately moved it to a lower one. If he priced a silver tray, she yanked off the tag and repriced it. They could not agree on which box to unpack next, and when she accidentally dropped a cut glass cream pitcher on the concrete floor, both the antique and the antique husband went all to pieces. Frustrations were unleashed by both of them and they began to go into rituals of practiced anger, many times before re-

hearsed. All those in neighboring booths were much relieved when he stalked out of the room in indignation.

Quietly she continued to set up the booth in anticipation for the next day's opening. One would have had to be blind not to see the glistening moisture streaking down her humiliated countenance. Nevertheless, the conflict was not acknowledged by either the sad old woman in Booth 307 nor by any of those in surrounding booths. The old man did not come back all day. No one knew where he was, nor did anyone really care, seemingly including the old woman. She was still there by herself when the other dealers left late in the afternoon. She just nodded her head when someone offered her a ride back to the motel.

It was good for Ruby to be by herself for a while. She and Larson had been married for over forty years. There was a lot of joy in those early years. They had respected one another and loved one another and pleased one another, but gradually something had happened. Now, they just seemed to irritate one another and cause discomfort. Both of them had forgotten their last wedding anniversary and any sort of gift-giving was a ritual they had mutually agreed to drop a long time ago. It was not either hatred or disgust that best described their feelings, but just trapped boredom. They had both grown too stubborn to sway with a situation and too tired to redeem a tarnished relationship.

The next morning when Ruby and Larson came in, the war was still raging. Hurtful phrases were thrust into the atmosphere until in a climactic moment both of them ran away from Booth 307. The neighbors did not know exactly what had happened, but time was drawing nigh for the show to open and no Ruby or Larson were to be seen. Did both of them expect the other to manage the booth? Even though neither of them arrived in time for the opening of the show, something else did.

A large bouquet of two dozen red roses was delivered from the florist shop in the lobby of the convention center. They were truly glamorous. Each bud seemed to hold a secret ready to be unfolded, and there was a card, a simple little card with hearts on a holder so that all could see. It read:

I TRULY LOVE YOU WITH ALL MY HEART.

Now anyone would be elated with such an array, and when Ruby came back to the booth, her slow steps began to pick up and when she picked up the card and read its text, her spirit and her face reflected that she had just had a deep drink at the fountain of youth. Brushing tears aside, she brushed her hair and more carefully did her face than she had in a long time. She began to smile and giggle and generate pleasure. By the time Larson found his way back to the booth, she was in full control of everything and she walked over to him, put her arms around him, and kissed him as if they were newlyweds. For a moment the startled old man looked as if he might faint. The neighboring dealers could not help but witness this display of affection. It was almost as embarrassing as the anger had been the day before, but they smiled and giggled with a bit of pleasure at the redemption.

The metamorphosis was an inspiration to watch. The old couple held hands and cooed all day long. There was, however, a strange facet to the story. Even though Ruby made it a point to show her friends and customers the note that accompanied the flowers, Larson told two of his friends that afternoon that it was the first time in his whole life that he had ever received flowers, and he actually beamed as he related to them the note that his wife had written to him. In fact, he told one customer that it was the best gift that Ruby had given him in the forty-two years they had been married.

So a little mystery began to arise among the neighbors. Did Ruby send the flowers to Larson, or did Larson send the flowers to Ruby? What genius was the motivating impetus for the miracle in Booth 307? Well, we simply do not know. That part of the story is missing. We probably never will know, nor do we need to know. It is enough to know about the redeeming qualities of love expressed.

It might have been noted by an observer that the dealer in the booth next to Booth 307 was seen paying a bill in the lobby florist shop the next morning.

The Greater Gift

$\mathscr{M}$artha listlessly wrapped some inane gift that she had bought for her mother. There was not much that seemed appropriate to give to someone who was in the hospital for her last Christmas. So many gifts, by their very implication of life, were almost cruel to present to someone who was flirting with death. It was that very awareness that probed the teenager to yearn for something special for her mother, something that would say what she could not bring her words to communicate. But what?

Martha looked at the formal hanging on the closet door. Everything was in readiness for the big dance that night, everything except Martha. It was the first party dress she had ever had that her mother had not made. Her father, in his own awkward way, had patiently spent hours shopping for the dress and had not even winced at the price. He had insisted on the satin shoes and purse dyed to match, which she knew they could not afford. Everyone was trying arduously for things to go right, but the undercurrent of a wrong illness flowed through them all. An excessive alterations charge had been made so that the hem of flowing fullness of the dress

would be just perfect. Maybe it was the thought of that alterations charge that made Martha hesitate and gasp a bit as she took a razor blade and began to rip the hem from the gorgeous garment.

She was hopeful that her task would be completed before her father returned home, but as he walked in about three o'clock, she ran into him in the front door. He looked askance and bewildered at the hemless dress in one of her arms, her curling irons, and a bag of God-knows-what in the other. She rushed by him pleading, "Trust me, Dad. Just trust me."

By five o'clock the hospital room looked as if the cyclone of Christmas had just swept through. The nursing supervisor had opened the door only once a little after four. She saw there a teenage girl, with her hair in rollers, standing on top of a night stand. A sick woman, who was supposed to have pills in her mouth, had pins instead and was desperately tugging at the hem of a dress.

The pills that the nurse had in her hand went into her pocket. The hand went a little deeper into the pocket, and she sent the aide to McDonald's for some hamburgers and fries. Then she put an ABSOLUTELY DO NOT DISTURB sign on the door and signed her name to it.

It was an ill-at-ease young man who walked down a hospital corridor with a corsage box in hand to pick up his date, but it was an at-ease-ill mother who greeted him at the door. Who knew her thoughts as she watched them board the elevator? Her smile was mysterious.

A weary mother sensed that she had just received as grand a gift as could ever be given, the sharing of life itself. It wasn't the sort of present that could be tied with a bow, but rather the sort that was bound by love. "Whosoever gives her life for my sake shall surely find it," a wise man once said. And a mother and daughter had surely found life as Christmas awesomely came in a hospital room of the evening of the Christmas prom.

A Door to Christmas

$\mathcal{I}$t was the fifth time that Bobby had walked past the door of the red brick house. The light snow caused the cup of hot chocolate he had treated himself to at the 7-Eleven to taste even better and it helped to warm his freezing hands. The house had a rather average look about it, except that there were no signs of Christmas. No lights, no tree, no wreath adorned the door. In fact, it looked as if no one lived there.

Once again the thirteen-year-old checked the address on the card that was in his pocket. Even though he had never met his maternal grandparents, he had certain expectations, which included being met at the bus station. He had envisioned having to be nice about loads of presents that were babyish and childish. He had planned to be aloof when they tried to hug and kiss him.

He was a rather somber youth, but the factors of his life were sobering. His mother had simply left three years ago and they had not heard from her. His father, who really wasn't a bad sort, just simply could not get his act together. This lack of self-control had finally landed him in jail. Thus it was that Bobby

had become a ward of the courts. Bobby had found the grandparents' address on a birthday card that was several years old, and since there were no other relatives, the court had made these hasty arrangements for Bobby to stay with his grandparents. So here he was, but wondering if the juvenile home might have been preferable.

The old man who answered the door was startled by Bobby's presence. They had not been notified when he was coming. There were no hugs. Just an awkward handshake and the admonition to, "Just call me Vernon." They walked through a living room obviously not used for living. The house was cold and dark, nothing at all as Bobby had imagined a real home would be. His grandmother was found in front of a TV in a worn-out room, which smelled of beer and cigarettes, but Bobby was used to that smell.

It was a strange and uncomfortable evening for all of them. Bobby was amused to sense their near fear of him. He was an interruption. They had developed a pattern of dying month by month. Their house was accompanying them in the degenerating process. They had closed and sealed the doors not only of most of the house, but on most of life as well. The hurt Bobby's mother had caused had been a key that locked out joy forever. Yet, here was this child who was their responsibility for at least six months. On the other hand, Bobby was more comfortable in that situation than he might have been had it been one of typical grandparenting.

The morning has more wisdom than does the

night. They discussed school at breakfast, and afterwards Bobby wandered into the big living room. The drapes were sewn together with cobwebs but scissored apart easily by the rays of the morning sun. A miracle of blue, gold, and purple rays designed themselves around the crystal bowl on the dining table. Bobby had never seen anything like it. His grandfather explained that it was cut glass and showed Bobby how the cuttings caught and turned the vectors of light into lasers of color. The old man casually mentioned that ammonia could make it sparkle as a bushel of diamonds.

Immediately Bobby went into the kitchen to search for some ammonia. "It's under the sink, but what in the world do you want with it?" his grandmother inquired. With great curiosity she came into the living room and was gratified to see his interest in the bowl. For an hour he polished off the accumulation of neglect the years had bestowed.

They were all gratefully relieved for something upon which they could focus together, so the bowl received an inordinate amount of attention. It had been a wedding gift to his grandmother's parents. She recalled the various functions at which it had been used over the years, but she commented that at Christmas it was always reserved for azaleas. "What's an azalea?" he had asked. Did you ever try to explain to a thirteen-year-old boy what an azalea was? It was not a bad morning for any of them.

After lunch Bobby went out. He had arrived with almost thirty-five dollars in his pocket. He could not help but grin as he reflected upon the irony of the situation. His grandparents needed him as much as he needed them. He had wondered about what they might give him, but never had the thought tickled his mind as to what he might give them. He simply had not considered ever wanting to begift them. Now he was in his third florist shop, trying to buy an azalea. They had tried to sell him all sorts of plants, but his heart was set on an azalea.

It was almost five o'clock when he knocked on the old, foreboding door for the second time in less than twenty-four hours. This time he was electrified with anticipation. His grandmother quickly brushed aside a tear because her heart understood what the azalea plant was communicating. Years of closed doors began to open in her soul. With tenderness, she placed the gift in the sparkling bowl, as she carefully and studiously circled the table three times. The flowers made a statement that beauty still existed and that caring was still a reality.

"Bobby, this bowl had some old friends with which it used to spend Christmas a long time ago. I think the time has come for a reunion. There is a chest of silver underneath the bed in which you slept last night and a tablecloth in the middle drawer of the buffet."

"Vernon," his wife directed, "take this list and go to the store."

"While he's gone, Bobby, all the crystal in this china cabinet needs to be washed."

"We haven't eaten in here in years," protested

the old man, as he stared at his wife with astonishment. He could hardly believe what he was seeing. Life was flowing again in eyes that had long since dulled. "It's been fifteen years since we had a Christmas dinner."

"Well, we are going to tonight if Christmas is not over by the time you get back from the store," she scolded, with a tenor in her voice that he had almost forgotten. And they did.

The aging couple had opened the door of their home and hearts to Bobby. On the other hand, he had opened the door to life for them. A wise teacher once taught, "Knock and it shall be opened for you." But the wise teacher could no longer say, "Behold, I stand at the door and knock," because in that home, the door of love had been pushed open, never to be closed again.